THE BUNBU

BUN NOEL

Text by David English
Pictures by Jan Brychta

FONTANA/Collins

For Lida Brychta

First published by Collins in 1989

First published in 1989 by Fontana Paperbacks
8 Grafton Street, London W1X 3LA

Copyright © David English and Jan Brychta, 1989

Printed in Great Britain by
Cambus Litho, East Kilbride

It was December in Bunbury. Bunnies' noses twitched as the cold light streamed through the bare trees. The branches, like rheumatic fingers, were silhouetted against the wintry sun, a stark contrast from the soft lush greens of summertime. Now, as the chill winds from the North whipped the snow in flurries and squalls through Sleepy Time Hollow, Old Holbun and his wife, Mary, were preparing their home for some very important visitors. Thoughtfully, they hung up the decorations, prepared the meal, and roasted chestnuts on a roaring fire.

In the centre of the room stood eleven empty chairs. But would the Bunburys be back to fill them in time for Christmas?

'Ah, Mary,' sighed Holbun, sinking into his favourite armchair, 'to think that just a few months ago Bunbury Green was bathed in sunshine: the sound of children playing, the ground ringed by chestnuts, and the lads competing against Mike Catting's Whiskertown in the Bunson & Hedges Cat West Final.'

'Yes, dear,' said Mary Holbun, soothingly. 'Now, drink up your Bunvita.'

On the other side of the world, Ian Buntham and Viv Radish were sunning themselves in the tropical paradise of Bunnybados. The cricket season had ended and they were enjoying a well-earned respite from battles on the field.

'This is the life, Viv,' sighed Buntham.

'Ya, man, cool,' replied Viv, gazing up at the trees.

'What are you doing?' said Buntham.

'Oh, nothing, man, just reading me palm.'

The level rays of the sun glittered on the smooth stems of the palm trees, throwing rainbows across the foam upon the coral reefs. Viv slipped into a dream.

So did Mary Holbun, day-dreaming in her cottage. Picking up a
sepia photograph, she looked wistfully at the chappie in the turbun.
Little Rajbun had made his passage back to India. After defeating the
Katman of Kathmandu, he had become a national hero. Elephants
linked tails to trunks in celebration, and swung happily along the
dusty roads. In the bazaars, traders sold beautiful silks bearing the
Bunbury colours, green, yellow and blue, and at Vindaloo Station the
little Rajbunnies sat atop the trains, singing and displaying their new
'Urdus'. Harry Sikhombe had written 'Rajbun's Theme' specially, and
all of India seemed to chant the young Bunbury's name.

At the same time, Dennis Lettuce and Rodney Munch were
winging their way back to Bunbury on Kookaburra Airways, flight
LBW2 via Bunkok and Singapaw. They had spent their holidays with
their pals, Dingo Den and Alice Springs at Hares Rock, lapping up the

Aussie sun. Poor Munch was nursing a headache. He had drunk one carrot juice too many and got thrown out of a bar in Brisbun or was it Melbun?

'Jeepers, pal, I feel poorly,' moaned Munch.

'Well, fancy stealing a boomerang up your pullover, mate,' said Dennis Lettuce.

'Yeah. I reckon I must have got thrown out of that bar 148 times . . . "Waltzing bewildered, waltzing bewildered, I'll come a waltzing bewildered with you",' he chanted.

'Nothing to declare, mate,' stumbled Munch on arrival at Buckteethrow. 'Just a headache.'

Old Holbun lit his pipe and scraped away the frost inside the window. The snow had formed iridescent whirls on the panes. As he pulled on his favourite tobacco, Olde Holbun, his thoughts began to crystallize. The last year had been eventful: beating Whiskertown

and their Caribbean superstar, Hattrick Catterson; saving the American baseball team, the Twitchita Tumblers from certain defeat. Graham Dillbunny and Philip de Fruit Bun had played particularly well.

At that moment, Dillbunny and de Fruit Bun were in Burrow-in-Ernest watching Rugby League. Huddled round the television they cheered excitedly between gulps of hot soup.

'That Jonabun Davies is a good player,' shouted Dillbunny. 'Go on, pass it on to the winger!'

'Give it to Bunny Robson!' yelled John Emberbunny from the director's box. Sir Matt Bunsby had invited Emberbunny and Cress Broadbun to Bunchester United to watch the game. He beamed happily at his beloved ground, only recently saved from the clutches of the dodgy developer Peter Rackbun. The place was packed for the crunch battle against Wimblebun FC. Bunchester had beaten the Bunners of Haresenal during the week, but Wimblebun were proving tougher hopposition. Vinny Buns passed to John Bashanu. Whack! went Paul McGrass. Penalty!

'Rubbish!' shouted Cress Broadbun. 'Never a penalty. What acting! Tell John Hurt to give him a BIFTA Award!'

Mike Catting and Graham Pooch had gone dog-racing at Catford. Crossing the track at half-time, they were chased by five energetic greyhounds and managed to clock a record time for the distance.

'Bloomin' dogs,' puffed Catting, 'wish they'd keep their traps shut!'

'Hang on,' panted Pooch. 'Look at the next two races. There's the Aussies from the Great Terrier Reef, Allan Bounder, Simon O'Doggal, Terry Doberman, Geoff Pawson and Dean Bones followed by Javed Miandog, Steve Wuff and our own Jack Russell.'

'Blow that' said Catting. 'We'll be safer at the Barkshire Golf Classic with Nick Fido, Jack Nicklaws and Seve Bunnysteros.'

Holbun and Mary curled up sleepily in their cosy cottage. Outside the air was thick with the cries of bobble-hatted juniors tumbling in the snow. Mittened kittens and bouncing bunnies skated happily through the icy fingers of the blizzard.

What a joy to see the happiness in a child's eye, thought Holbun. Who cares about runny noses and chapped lips? Just the boundless pleasure of sliding, gliding toboggan dreams, watched by the snowman who seems . . . to see everything . . . then the long trek homewards . . .

'Come on, dear. Wake up. You're nodding off again,' whispered Mary kindly.

Alan Ram and Goldenhare were also enjoying the snow over in Val D'Ishare.

'Come on, Goldenhare, I'll beat you down the Cresta Bun!' cried Ram.

Ian Buntham and Viv Radish looked lazily out to sea. They could hear the waves crashing against the reef like rolling thunder. Then suddenly, the skies darkened and clouds began to roll over the angry waters of the bay.

'Hurricane!' screamed an old lady.

But it was too late. There had been no warning. Ian and Viv were up in a flash, carrying children from the beach and lifting the elderly beyond the palms. But there had been no time to sound the island's alarms. No hurricane reports had been broadcast on television or radio. It had struck with the suddenness that makes all hurricanes so terrifying. In a few moments of violence it had irrevocably changed hundreds of lives.

'Down! Lie down on the ground!' yelled Buntham, his arms around the heads of two kids. But the hurricane showed no respect. It ripped into the rum shacks and swirled around the homes. Pedaloes from the beach were blown for miles, their brightly coloured sails ripped to shreds. The residents of the towns dotted about Bunnybados desperately sought shelter, but were quickly drenched by the rains as the streets became waterlogged.

'The sky is crying,' sang Viv sadly. 'Look at the tears rolling down the street.'

Then, in the middle of the holocaust, an eerie calm settled on the island.

'Look up there, Viv,' hollered Buntham.

A terrible yellow eye had pierced the darkness, and a voice boomed out of the sky, 'Bunnybados, you are finished. Bunburys beware, I will be back. Roary has spoken!'

Then, in a final explosion, the eye vanished as suddenly as it had appeared.

Peering through the snow flurry, Old Holbun could just make out two lights slicing the gloom. 'Look, Mary, it must be a couple of shooting stars!'

As the two bunnies watched, the lights drew closer and closer, brighter and brighter, and then the whole cottage shuddered as the dark shadow zoomed overhead. It was the Bunnymobile, and as it dipped and rolled in a victory salute, they could just make out the pilot's features. There was Goldenhare Gower, grinning all over his face. Behind him sat Allan Ram, John Emberbunny, Philip de Fruit Bun, Rodney Munch, Graham Dillbunny, Cress Broadbun, Dennis Lettuce and Rajbun.

Within the hour, Holbun's cottage was alive with the sounds of merriment and bunhomie. The nine Bunburys sat around happily exchanging stories and enjoying the reunion. But still there were two empty chairs.

'It's no good,' said Holbun. 'The team is incomplete. What could be keeping Ian and Viv?'

'Look,' said Goldenhare. 'There's a news flash on the television.'

As the Bunburys crammed round the set, Ian McCatskill's furrowed fur lit up the screen.

'Today the island of Bunnybados was almost totally destroyed by the evil Hurricane Roary. The place is devastated; the people are in shock. The hurricane has severed all power and telephone lines, and people have lost their homes . . . Over to you, Trevor Macderbun.'

'Hello, Ian. Well, here I am in that little England in the tropic seas, amongst the debris, and with me is the mayor of Bunnybados.'

'Ya, man. Well, one moment I was in me home in Bridgetown, the next I was perched on de cliffs at Ragged Point. It is terrible. De cricket ground is flooded and next week we got de crucial Shell Shield game against Tobungo.'

'Talking of cricket,' interrupted Macderbun, 'we have two of the famous Bunburys on the island: Viv Radish and Ian Buntham.'

'Look, it's Beefy!' cried Rajbun. By now the Bunburys were glued to the screen as their pals explained their plight.

'We're all marooned here on Bunnybados. The island is stricken with terror as the hurricane has threatened to return. If our team mates are watching, please help, fellas. This is an SOS, repeat, SOS . . .'

The picture became distorted and finally faded.

In a trice, Old Holbun's cottage was emptied. The door swung on its hinges, letting in an icy draft. Slowly, a tear in her eye, Mary took the mince pies out of her oven.

'Oh well, Mary dear,' she said to herself, 'business comes before pleasure. Do take care, lads. Come back safely.'

The cottage shook as the Bunnymobile flew overhead, destination Bunnybados.

It was midnight before the Bunburys circled the ravaged island. The mottled moon in troubled skies picked out Tranquil Town on the north side of Bunnybados. Goldenhare landed skilfully, in a sugarcane field flattened by the terrible winds.

'Maybe the islanders can start a new sugar,' said Dennis Lettuce. 'Call it Hurry Cane.'

'They might have to,' murmured Munch gloomily.

'Right,' said Old Holbun, 'we'll continue on foot. Let's find Ian and Viv. They'll be staying with the mayor.'

The mayor's residence stood in Flamboyant Avenue. At least, it used to. Half of it was scattered all over Sunset Crest; the other half was still standing and had been turned into a hospital. Nurses and doctors were tending the injured whilst little children walked aimlessly through the rubble, searching for their mothers.

Buntham and Radish, their sleeves rolled up, lifted and carried, encouraged and soothed the homeless and invalid. Then, in the half-light of a hurricane lamp, Viv caught sight of Old Holbun. 'Hey man, over here! Boy, it's good to see you!' beamed the Bunnybadian.

With gladdened hearts the Bunburys embraced their chums and once again the team was united.

In the morning, the mayor led the Bunburys through Tranquil Town. They stopped where a car had been blown off the road into a tree. Its rear windows were gone.

'There's a lady in here,' called out Dillbunny, inspecting the wreck. Carefully, he helped the woman out of the front seat.

'Here's a little kitten lying in the back,' piped up Rajbun. 'It's all wet.'

'Don't worry,' said Ram to the lady, 'we'll take care of your cat.'

'But I don't have a cat,' replied the woman.

Just then, a fellow came walking down the street holding two other kittens. 'Hey, man, you haven't seen me third kitty?'

The look of joy on his face when Ram held out the dripping kitten was wondrous to behold.

'What happened to you?' enquired Philip de Fruit Bun to an old man.

'Well, man, I tell you. I was sitting on de outside toilet. You got to be fast or you get de chapped legs. Know what I mean?'

'Of course,' nodded de Fruit Bun.

'Well, blow me if one moment I was sitting there and de next I was plonk in de middle of de church assembly, five miles away in Speightstown. Very embarrassing, man, I can tell you!'

All day the Bunburys listened to the islanders' tales of woe.

'Help me! Help me!' cried an old lady.

'What's wrong?' said Buntham.

'Two of me children, Desmond and Violet, were sleeping beside me. Lucy was in de other room. I looked out de window and saw me garage flying across de backyard. Me heart froze. I tried to go and get Lucy, but I never made it.'

'Calm down, Missis,' said Buntham.

'I can't calm down,' she cried. 'The windows shattered, the bedroom floor tilted and the ceiling collapsed. Next ting I knew, I was outside in de rain, struggling to see without me glasses. Desmond and Violet are okay, but I've lost Lucy. I can't find my baby!'

'Cool it, ma'am,' said Viv, gently. 'Holbun, can you please look after this lady?'

Old Holbun put a blanket around the lady's shoulders and comforted her while the Bunburys searched for the little girl. It proved a surreal search: carpets had draped themselves round trees, great slabs of roofing lay upside down, and furniture stood askew in back gardens. In the middle of the road someone spotted the crib in which Lucy had been sleeping. It was terribly twisted and lay under mounds of rubble. The Bunburys dashed over and began pushing back the debris, desperate to find the child.

'Over here!' cried Emberbunny.

He had found Lucy. She was wrapped snugly in her mattress, unharmed except for a few scratches.

'She's alive,' sang a happy Radish. 'Viv and let Viv!'

That evening the Bunburys and the mayor called an emergency meeting.

'We must be ready for the hurricane,' said Buntham. 'I have an idea. What's tomorrow, Viv?'

'Sunday,' replied Radish.

'Right, let's get cracking. Tomorrow will be Palm Sunday.'

Everybody worked hard through the night, following Buntham's directions.

'We'll tie the palms back and make catapults. Soon see if that hurricane is coconut shy!'

Early the next morning, there was a cry from the lookout. 'There it is!'

Sure enough, far out in the bay, the hurricane was gathering speed, tearing through the sky towards the island.

'Steady!' screamed Buntham above the din. 'When I say fire, aim for its eye! Now!'

As the hurricane passed overhead, the Bunburys fired a volley of coconuts, one salvo after the other. But it was no good, the hurricane simply closed its eye and the coconuts rapped its lid harmlessly, causing it to laugh raucously.

'It's no good, Bunburys. You'll have to be smarter than that!'

'To the Bunnymobile!' ordered Old Holbun.

Quickly the lads climbed in and took off. Flying over the bay, Holbun shouted, 'Viv, get on one wing, Ian the other. Goldenhare, hold the mobile steady. You'll only get one chance. Viv, take your bat and Ian, bowl when I say.'

Meanwhile, the hurricane had turned to take another destructive swipe at Bunnybados. It tore towards the Bunnymobile now hovering over a raging sea. Then strangely, it stood still, pirouetting like a matador before its kill. Viv stood as steadily as he could, holding his bat. The eye of the hurricane peered fiercely down on him.

'Bowl now, Ian!'

Buntham steadily bowled right arm over to his mighty Bunnybadian pal. Viv smashed the ball and it flew like an arrow through the storm. The Bunburys looked on for a seemingly endless moment. Then, *crash*! The ball went straight into the evil eye. It recoiled, blinked frantically and finally closed. The bruised skies dissolved and an air of peace and calm descended upon Bunnybados.

When the Bunburys landed, they were garlanded and cheered by the islanders.

'You're very kind,' said Buntham. 'But the job isn't finished! You must be ready for Tobungo tomorrow.'

'But de ground is flooded,' lamented the mayor.

'Yes,' agreed Buntham, winking at Viv, 'but all is not lost.'

When the Tobungo cricket team arrived, they made their way to the Kensington Oval.

'What can we play?' enquired the Tobungo skipper. 'Underwater cricket?'

'Not exactly,' laughed the Bunburys. 'Let's see what you're like at water sports!'

For one glorious day, the Bunnybadians tried to forget the state of their stricken island. Watching the two teams competing at waterskiing and wind surfing, they cheered happily, 'Come on Viv, come on lads!'

At the end of a sun-splashed afternoon, Old Holbun led his team to the Bunnymobile. But before he could leave a little girl rushed out to him from the crowd and cried, 'What can we do now? Our island is wrecked!'

'Don't worry,' sympathised Old Holbun. 'We have some very special friends in England who will help. You are brave people. If we work together as a team we can repair your homes and your lives.'

The mayor and his people waved fondly as the Bunnymobile took off from the tropical island.

'Now, we must make three very important phone calls,' said Old Holbun. 'Rajbun, get me Mr Albert Hall on the bunny phone.'

As Goldenhare steered the Bunnymobile homewards, Old Holbun spoke commandingly. 'Hello, Albert. We will want to hire your hall on New Year's Eve. Get me the Bunbury band together . . . 7.30 pm start . . .

'Hello Frances. Alert the *Bugle*. I want headlines!'

Loosening his collar, Holbun made his last call.

'Yes, dear . . . All is well . . . Mission half completed . . . Get those mince pies ready . . . Yes . . . What? . . . Yes, I love you too, dear.'

'Sssh! Close the gate,' whispered Buntham.

Stealthily the Bunburys and their manager tiptoed up the path to Old Holbun's cottage. The door was open. Inside the embers of the dying fire still glowed. The eleven chairs were empty and there, dozing in her hubby's armchair, was Mary. In her hands she clasped a photo of her beloved team. Her dreams fell into darkness as two massive hands covered her eyes.

'Wake up, Mary!' shouted Ian and Viv.

'Merry Christmas!' sang the Bunburys.

Mary Holbun stirred and immediately burst into tears. 'My boys! My boys!' she cried between hugs and kisses.

On New Year's Eve, the Bunbury band of Eric Clapbun, Bunny, Robun and Maurice Gibb, George Hare-ison and Elton Bun played to a capacity crowd in Albert's Hall in London.

Thousands of pounds were raised and duly despatched to Bunnybados, and after months of hard work, the Bunnybadians restored their island to its former sparkling glory.

If you visit Tranquil Town you will find a street called Bunbury Way where kids play without fear in their hearts. By the side of the street there is a little stone. Its inscription reads:

A Bunbury stands for freedom
Stands for fun
Stands for ever being young.
So do a good turn unto others,
Never turn from your quest,
For you are a Bunbury
And a Bunbury does his best!

David English has always been a cricket fanatic.
At the age of seventeen he was so engrossed in a match taking
place on the other side of the road that he failed to notice
an oncoming car and was run over.
He decided that hospital was not for him,
and with a fellow patient ran off to
Africa on 25 shillings, missing his A levels in the process.

In the early seventies he worked for Robert Stigwood,
managing stars like the Bee Gees and Eric Clapton before
deciding to become an actor. He has just produced
his first feature film with Barry Gibb, entitled *Hawks*.

He is now a member of the MCC and plays cricket
for Middlesex CCC, Cross Arrows, Finchley CC and the EC XI.
He first worked with Jan Brychta presenting *You and Me* for the BBC.

Jan Brychta is a Czechoslovakian-born, award-winning artist
who has worked as a designer and illustrator on
a number of BBC television programmes for children such as
Jackanory, *Play School* and *Music Time*.
Exhibitions of his work
have now been held in Germany, France, Norway and the UK.
Jan says he must be the first Czech ever to understand a maiden over.